EVERYTHING
HAS A PLACE

BY PATRICIA LILLIE
PICTURES BY NANCY TAFURI

GREENWILLOW BOOKS · NEW YORK

Watercolor paints and a black pen were used
for the full-color art.
The text type is Helvetica Rounded Bold and
Burt Bold.

Printed in Hong Kong by South China Printing
Company (1988) Ltd.
First Edition   10 9 8 7 6 5 4 3 2 1

Library of Congress Cataloging-in-Publication Data
Lillie, Patricia.
   Everything has a place / by Patricia Lillie ;
pictures by Nancy Tafuri.
       p.   cm.
   Summary: Text and pictures assign a cow to a barn,
a dish to a cupboard, a family to a house,
and other things to their place.
   ISBN 0-688-10082-1. ISBN 0-688-10083-X (lib. bdg.)
   I. Tafuri, Nancy, ill.   II. Title.
PZ7.L632Er   1993
[E]—dc20   90-23497   CIP   AC

For JessiAnn
—P. L.

For Cristina
—N. T.

A cow
in a
barn,

a bird
in a nest,

a flower
in a garden,

a dish
in a
cupboard,

a cat
in a chair,

a teddy
on a bed,

a book
on a
shelf,

a crayon
in a box,

a fish
in a bowl,

a baby on
a lap,

a family in a house.

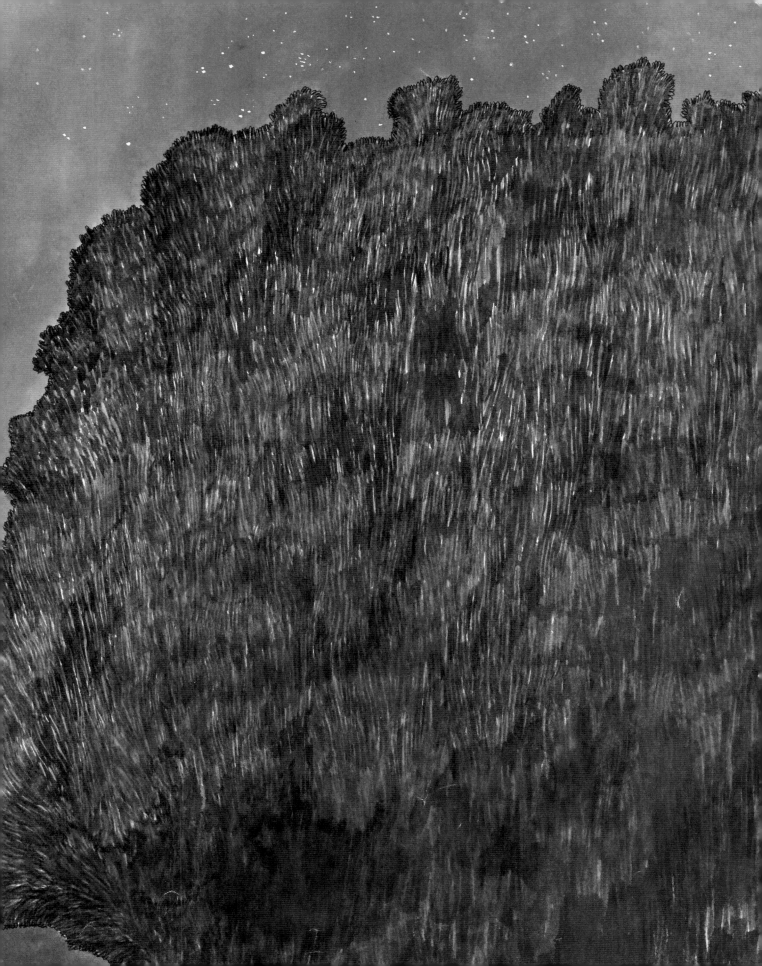